KESO TALES

≈ The Adventures Of An African American Slave Girl In South Carolina ≈

**by Kitty Wilson-Evans
and Lucinda R. Dunn**

illustrations by Jason Curry

I live to tell the story.
– KWE

To Sammy, from mommy with love.
– LRD

ISBN: 0-9819007-0-4
ISBN-13: 9780981900704

Visit www.booksurge.com to order additional copies.

FOREWORD

Slavery is a practice in which one person owns another person. From 1618 to 1865, Africans and their descendants were enslaved in colonial America and the United States. For the first time in history, enslavement was based solely on skin color. Before the widespread establishment of chattel slavery, much labor was organized under a system of bonded labor known as indentured servitude. This typically lasted for several years for white and black alike, and it was a means of using labor to pay the costs of transporting people to the colonies. By the 1700's court rulings established the racial basis of the American incarnation of slavery to apply chiefly to African and people of African descent, and occasionally to Native Americans. Since the Southern colonies needed more resources than in the North due to their labor-intensive tobacco culture, the ratio of slaves in the South was higher. Slaves were treated as property and had no rights. A person born into slavery was a slave for life. The life of a slave was very different from the one of a free person. Slaves worked long and hard. Slaves who disobeyed could be severely punished. Slaves were forbidden to read and write. If slaves were caught trying to improve themselves, they would be punished. In addition, slaves could be sold from one master (owner) to another.

Kessie's Tales: The adventures of an African American Slave Girl in South Carolina is a fictional account of one young, slave girl's life and adventures living on a South Carolina plantation.

Special thanks to:

My daughters

My family and friends

South Carolina Arts Commission
(Lancaster)

Barbara McKinnon

Dori Sanders

D. Lindsay Pettus

Samuel and Alice Dunn

———————

In memory of:

Marjorie McMurray

KESSIE'S TALES:

The Adventures of an
African-American Slave Girl

Kitty Wilson-Evans and Lucinda R. Dunn
Illustrations by Jason Curry

Kessie and the Good Shoes

Kessie, a young slave girl, worked in the fields and was often called to help care for her master and missus' children.

One day, Kessie was sent to the Big House to care for master and missus' baby girl in the nursery. She overheard the master telling his wife that if Kessie were going to care for their children, she would need the proper clothing. Kessie would need a new frock and a pair of good shoes to wear.

Kessie looked down at her old battered shoes. They looked just fine to her. She could not understand why the master was making such a fuss over her shoes. Besides, her frock covered them anyhow.

Now right before "the big times"—what the slaves called Christmas—the master called for Kessie to come up to the Big House. When Kessie arrived at the house, she was told by one of the house servants that the master was waiting for her in the study.

Kessie walked into the big room. Her master was sitting at his desk and on the desk was a big box.

Her master looked up from the paper he had in his hands. "Come in child, come in. Do you have any idea why I have sent for you?"

"No sir. Master, did I do something wrong?" Kessie answered.

"No Kessie," her master answered, "but I need to see the shoes you are wearing."

Kessie closed her eyes. There he goes again she thought, talking about my shoes. She raised the hem of her frock to show her master the old shoes she was wearing.

"Kessie, I have a gift for you. Since your missus needs your help in the nursery, you must wear the proper clothing. Your missus will give you a new frock. I have for you a fine pair of shoes. They came all the way from up north." The master handed the box to Kessie, and told her that when she came for her duties in the nursery the next morning, he expected her to wear her good shoes.

Kessie thanked her master and returned to the quarters. On the way back, with the box under her arm and walking down the dusty road to the cabin all she could think about was how much she loved her old battered shoes and how good they felt on her feet.

When Kessie opened the door of the cabin, her brother James asked her if she was in any trouble. Kessie told him no, that the master had given her a gift, a pair of good shoes made up north. Now her brother knew how much Kessie loved her old shoes and wondered what she was going to do now that she was told she had to wear the good shoes.

Kessie started to cry, "James, what am I going to do? You know how much these shoes mean to me. These were Ma's shoes. Remember before Ma died she gave me her old shoes. She told me that whenever I wear them to think of her and how much she loves me. When I wear Ma's old shoes it makes me feel like she is right here with me all through the day, whether I am in the fields or up at the Big House. Now I'm told that I can't wear them anymore."

James put his arms around his sister and told her not to cry, that their Ma would not want her to be unhappy. James was older and his Ma had made him promise to take care of his little sister, and he had tried to keep that promise.

"Kessie, listen to me. No matter where we are, Ma is with us. Just because you can't wear her shoes when you are working up at the Big House doesn't mean Ma wouldn't understand. Besides, don't you know Ma understands why you have to dress proper when you are needed in the nursery? She would not want you to get in trouble 'cause of her old shoes. Ma knows you have to obey the master and the missus. Did the master tell you to give him your old shoes?"

Kessie thought for a minute and said, "No, he didn't."

"See Chile, you get to keep Ma's shoes, and you get a brand new pair of shoes too. Just think about it Kessie, now you got two pair of shoes. When you go to work in the nursery, you wear the good shoes. Down here in the quarter and in the fields, you can wear Ma's shoes. Seems like to me you are blessed. Not many slaves on the plantation can say they have two pair of shoes. Not even me."

Kessie smiles. Her brother gives her a big hug, and looks on as his sister takes the shoes out of the box.

"All right, now try them on and let me see how Kessie looks in her good shoes!"

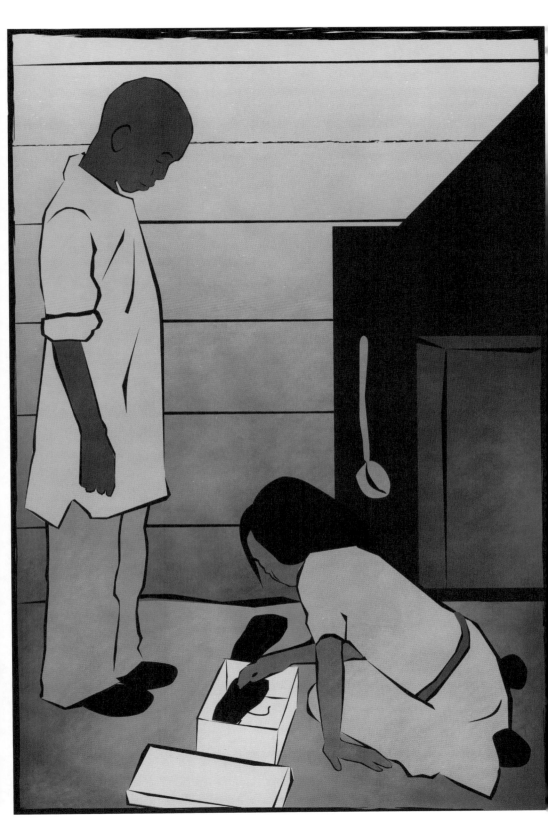

Celebrating the Big Times

Merry Christmas to all. It's December, and this is the time of the year that everybody is excited and getting ready for the big day. There are presents and gifts. There is lots of work that we slaves have to do to help decorate the Big House. We decorate it with red ribbon and fresh greenery. The men folk get to white wash the walls, wash the windows and scrub the floors while making sure that everything is just like the master and missus wants.

All of us slaves are busy from sun up until late at night. The women cook and bake food for the master and his family. We also sew frocks for the missus and her daughters.

When we are finished with our work up at the Big House, we go back to the slave quarters. The missus has given us some of the leftover greenery and ribbon. We use it to decorate the doors and windows on our cabins.

We slaves, we look forward to this time of year

too. We call it the "Big Times". You see, the "Big Times" is when we get the extra food and the new clothes for the year. But what we are thankful for is we get five days off to spend with our families. There isn't any working for the master and missus. The time is spent with our family members. We get a pass from the master to go visit family members on other nearby plantations. Also, our families get a pass from their masters to come visit us here on this plantation.

All of us slaves look forward to this time, and we try very hard to make it special. We make the dolls and other toys for our children, and we play games. The men folk go out hunting for rabbit, possum, and squirrel. Yes sir, the cooking is very good. We women folk get the wild greens, and we have sweet potatoes and ham hocks to cook.

There will be dancing, singing and story telling for the "Big Times." There are stories about Bro. Rabbit, Anansie the spider, and the baby Jesus and how he comes to save all his children. When the fiddle starts to play, we all get ready to dance the Juba and the pigeon wing. Yes sir, it is a real happy time spent with our loved ones. A time to be thankful that we are all together for another "Big Times" celebration.

But there is something all us slaves have on our

minds. We try not to think about it, but it is there. What kind of year did the master have? Was it a good one? Will he need extra money? And if that is the case, will he need to sell some of us? We can't help but think about what is going to happen. However, for now, we are just going to be thankful. We are all here as a family once again celebrating the "Big Times."

The Country Slave in the City

Kessie, a plantation slave from South Carolina journeys with her owner Henrietta Ivey to Charleston, South Carolina to visit one of the Ivey's daughters who is attending Miss Dupree's Girls' Academy. The day Miss Ivey prepares to return to her plantation, Kessie is told she will not be returning with her missus. Instead, she will stay in Charleston to serve Miss Agnes.

For this plantation slave, the days and months traveling with her young missus around Charleston and then to Savannah, Georgia will become an adventure she will never forget. You see, Kessie will become a part of the city slave's way of life. How will this South Carolina plantation slave adapt to her new surroundings?

Listen as Kessie shares with you another way of life for a slave—the city slave as seen through the eyes of a country slave.

Ya'll I just have to tell you what happened to me a long time ago when I was younger than I am now.

All ya'll know I am a plantation slave here in South Carolina. It is a mighty big plantation way out in the country. You don't get to leave here for nothing. Everything we slaves need is right here on this plantation.

Now missus and master have some girls. I hear that the missus is going to visit one of her daughters down in Charleston, South Carolina. The daughter is at the Miss Dupree's Girl Academy. Now the missus calls me up to the Big House and tells me I am going with her on this journey to visit her daughter. I don't know how long she is going to stay and when she is coming back home.

On this journey to Charleston, I see so much that I have never seen in my whole life. I see streets and all the buildings. And there are slaves walking the streets right in the middle of the day!

The missus is so happy to visit her child. We haven't been there long, and one day the missus tells me that she is going back to the master and the other members of her family because they need her on the plantation. She tells me, "Kessie you need to stay here. You will not be returning right now. Miss Agnes (that's her daughter's name) needs you to tend to her needs." Oh, Lord, what can I do? I need to get back to my family. They think that I will be traveling back with

the missus when she returns, but now I don't know when I will see my family again.

***

I have traveled many days and months with my young missus all around Charleston and then down to Savannah, Georgia. I have met slaves there and asked them about life for them there in the city. The stories they have told me are hard for me to believe and understand. One day I met this slave by the name of Diana. And she told me a whole lot about slave life in the city. For the life of me, I just can't believe all that she has told me. For one thing, the city slave's work is a whole lot different. They work what is called the task system. Your master and missus give you a task to do, like mending or sewing, and when you get finished with that task you are free to go back to your quarters, which is over the carriage house in the back of the big house in the city. The city slaves can now do chores for themselves, like mainly things for their family.

Back on the plantation, we slaves work from can to can't. We don't stop until the overseer tells us to stop. The overseer, he is the man that watches over all the slaves on the plantation. Here in the city, if the master

or missus needs something from the market place, the slaves go into the city to buy what they need.

But what a real lesson for me about the city slave's life is that the city slaves can take some of the things they have made during their free time and sell it at the Market place. The money they get from selling, they get to keep it for the family.

I get to go into the city with Diana and what these old eyes get to see, I will never forget. There are free slaves, run-aways, and so many more hiring themselves out for work to the different folks at the market. Not many of the slaves can read or write because that is against the law for us to sit and get learning. The only reason I can read and write is that for a long time when my master and missus had the Ivey Girls Academy, I was the slave down there helping the head missus. Here in the city, they call the head missus a teacher.

My young missus has just called me to come to her room. She tells me to start packing her belongings and that it is time for us to return to Charleston now that the holiday visit is over. Her mother will meet her there when we return.

Ya'll, I sure am happy to hear this good news because the young missus says to me that her mother said to

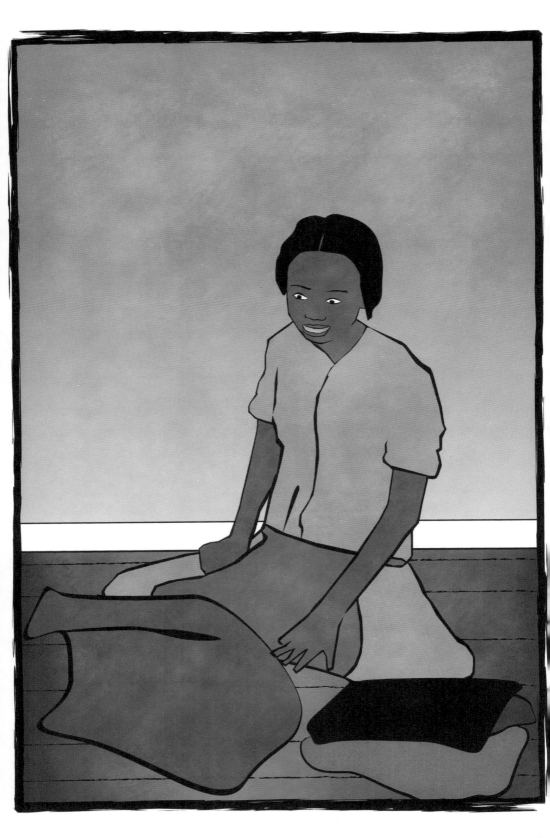

let old Kessie know that she will be traveling back to South Carolina with her. Those are happy words to my ears. I am going back to my family on the plantation. I pray that I won't ever have to make another journey like this ever again.

The family and home is very important to all slaves, even if it is a plantation out in the country in South Carolina.

Kessie's Little Thumb Baby

One day Kessie was all alone in the herb garden. She had been sent out there to pull all the weeds from around the young herb plants. She was told not to leave until her work was done.

Oh, how Kessie wished that one of the other slave children had been sent out there with her. That way the work would be done much faster. Besides, her fingers were sore from pulling all the weeds.

Kessie looked at her pointer finger and thumb. Oh, they hurt so much. She bent her fingers up and down. She wiggled her thumb towards her face. And guess what? By wiggling her thumb up and down it was as if her thumb was trying to talk to her, just like the puppets the master's children enjoyed in the nursery. "Are you trying to tell me something, Thumb?" "Yes, I am. When you get lonesome or tired, just look at me and talk to me. I am always here and will listen to you all day long."

"Thank you, Thumb." Kessie tore a small piece of rag from her neckerchief and tied it around her thumb. "You are not just my thumb; you are my very own Thumb baby."

COLOR KESSIE'S
LITTLE THUMB BABY

About Kitty Wilson Evans

Kitty Wilson Evans was born in Ft. Benning, GA. Her last two years of high school were spent in Europe where she studied at the Heidelberg Conservatory of Music. She performed in Bach and Mozart festivals and as a recording artist. Later, she returned to Europe for her studies, spending a total of 11 years abroad. She has a BA from USC, Columbia and an MA from Winthrop University in Children's Literature.

Ms. Evans has been a performer in rural schools with the SC Arts Commission. As a teacher, she worked with the Chapter I in Lancaster Public Schools and as a professional teacher in private schools.

Ms. Evans is a well-known storyteller and slave interpreter throughout the Southeast where she frequently travels to countless events and festivals. Most recently, she was an African American interpreter at the Cumberland Gap Trades Fair in Kentucky. The event attracted 7,000 visitors.

In May 2000, Ms. Evans joined the staff of the York County Culture and Heritage Commission as a storyteller and interpreter at Historic Brattonsville. Less than ten years ago, she made history as a volunteer with her impersonation of enslaved African American lifeways at Historic Brattonsville plantation. Since that beginning, she has worked with staff and attracted other African Americans to the program. In 1998, the education programs at Historic Brattonsville won the prestigious Award of Merit from the American Association of State and Local History, in part due to the program on enslaved African Americans for school groups and the public.

Ms. Evans works with school programs, public programs and most recently under grant funding to take programs to preschoolers in Lancaster and Chester counties. The Close Foundation and Oninova Solutions, Inc funded these grants.

Kitty Wilson Evans lives in Lancaster, South Carolina and is the mother of two adult daughters. For more information, visit www.KessiesTales.com.

About Lucinda R. Dunn

The road Lucinda Dunn took to becoming a writer began in Georgia with the dream of becoming a publisher. She left Georgia with the promise of a banking career but with a purpose in her heart to write. Within one month of her move, she followed her heart and dream of becoming a publisher. The Rock Hill Runway Newspaper was born under her company Dunn Deal Publishing. Visit http://www.TheRockHillRunway.com

Lucinda decided to make the newspaper a unique, quality, business publication that would take the country by storm. In less than 9 months, she began reaching her goal. The paper is distributed in 12 states and growing. Lucinda has had the privilege to interview a Tuskegee Airman, a renowned historian, celebrities, and other known personalities. However, she is most proud that her company is helping to bridge the training gap for those businesses that need a new, fresh approach to business solutions. From writing in her journal and now on to owner, publisher, and editor-in-chief of Dunn Deal Publishing and The Rock Hill Runway, respectively, Lucinda is excitedly working on new novels and works.

Lucinda R. Dunn currently resides in South Carolina and is the mother of one son. For more information, contact www.DunnDealPublishing.com .

About Jason Curry

Jason Curry is a graphic and web designer, who does freelance design work in the Charlotte metropolitan area. He graduated from the University of South Carolina with a degree in Graphic Design with a cognate in African-American Studies. He resides in Lancaster, SC with his seven-year-old daughter. Visit http://www.currymedia.info/